V05

Summer Surprise

The Adventures of Callie Ann

Summer Surprise
The Ballet Class Mystery

Summer Surprise

Shannon Mason Leppard

BETHANY HOUSE PUBLISHERS 2/97
MINNEAPOLIS, MINNESOTA 55438

Summer Surprise
Copyright © 1997
Shannon Mason Leppard

Cover illustration by Sergio Giovine
Story illustrations by Toni Auble

Published by Bethany House Publishers
A Ministry of Bethany Fellowship, Inc.
11300 Hampshire Avenue South
Minneapolis, Minnesota 55438

Printed in the United States of America.

Library of Congress Cataloging-in-Publication Data

Leppard, Shannon Mason.
    Summer surprise / Shannon Mason Leppard.
        p.m . —(The adventures of Callie Ann ; book 1)
    Summary: While unhappily trying to accept God's plan to move her family to another town, Callie fears that everyone has forgotten her ninth birthday.
        ISBN 1–55661–813–1 (pbk.)
        [1. Moving, Household—Fiction. 2. Christian life—Fiction] I. Title. II. Series: Leppard, Shannon Mason. Adventures of Callie Ann ; book 1.
PZ7.L5565Su   1996
[Fic]—dc21   96–45833
                                                    CIP
                                                    AC

To Donn, my husband and best friend.
Thank you.

For our girls, Natalie and Jordan.
You both are wonderful. I love you.

Also, for Lois Gladys Leppard.
Where do I start to thank you?
I love you lots!

SHANNON MASON LEPPARD grew up in a small town in South Carolina, where summer days were spent under the shade of an old weeping willow tree and winters under the quilting frames of her grandmother. Shannon brings her flair for drama and make-believe to THE ADVENTURES OF CALLIE ANN, her first series with Bethany House. She and her husband, Donn, make their home in North Carolina along with their two teenage daughters.

Chapter One

"CALLIE ANN, WILL YOU PLEASE come downstairs?" Callie's mom shouted up the steps.

"I'm on my way," Callie called back. "I need to brush Miss Kitty first." Callie was trying not to hurry as she brushed the big black cat. She did not want to go to the new church. She wanted to go back to Greenville—back to where Meghan and Mr. Kitty and Grandmama and Papa were. Back home. Not here in Cornelius where she didn't know anybody.

"Callie Ann Davies, last call," Mom called again.

"Oh no, Miss Kitty," Callie said to her sleepy cat. "Mom sounds like she's getting mad." She put the brush down and went to the door. "OK, Mom, I'm coming."

As Callie came down the steps, her mother stared. "Callie Ann, what did you do—or should I say what *didn't* you do to your hair?" She turned Callie around, looking at Callie's curly red hair.

Callie could tell by the look on Mom's face that she didn't like the new hairstyle.

"But, Mom, I really like to wear my hair up," Callie said. "Meghan said I look older with it like this."

"Older than what, Callie? You're eight!" Mom pointed upstairs. "Go right back up to your room and brush your hair. And don't take long. We have to be at church in twenty minutes."

"Mom will never understand," Callie said to Miss Kitty back in her room. "Besides, I'll be nine in a few days. Isn't anybody going to remember that? Mom and Daddy always made a big deal out of birthdays when we were in Greenville."

Back home they had always given Callie a pot with three red tulips. Behind their house, Callie had had a garden of just birthday tulips. All twenty-four had come back this year.

Did anybody here even know Callie Ann Davies was having a birthday this week?

❧❧❧

Callie was very quiet all the way to church. Looking out the window of the car, she could see all the way downtown. This place was so small. Mom even said Callie could walk to school. Back home she would be on a bus with all her friends.

At the end of the morning service, Reverend Snow asked everyone to please welcome Reverend and Mrs. Davies and their children, David and *Kelly*.

"Mom, he doesn't even know my name!" Callie complained in a loud whisper. "Reverend Callen knew my name. I don't like it here. I want to go back home!"

"Callie Ann," Daddy said in a stern voice, "we *are* at home. Home is where your family is, and we're all here—you, me, David, and your mom. I'll be taking over as pastor in a few weeks. We needed to get here early so I could go over a few things with Reverend Snow."

Callie started to object. "But, Daddy—"

"No buts, Callie. We will make the best of it," Mom said.

David wasn't having any trouble making new friends. He was almost seventeen and really cute. At least, that's what the teenage girls always said. All the girls at church were talking to him. Nobody was talking to Callie.

Outside after church while Mom and Daddy were talking, Callie looked around for someone her age. All she could see were older kids, except one boy with wheat-colored hair. He might be about her age. But a *boy*!

Callie picked up Miss Kitty as soon as they got home from church. She held her close. "Oh, Miss Kitty, I really want to go back to Greenville. Back home."

After lunch, Mom and Daddy were going for a walk around town. They wanted to meet some of the people from church. "Would you like to walk with us, Callie? We could stop for ice cream," Daddy said as he gave Callie a hug.

"No, sir," Callie said in a sad voice. "Miss Kitty and I are going to stay in our room and write to Meghan and Mr. Kitty."

"If you're sure then. We won't be gone long.

David is in the backyard with Jenni Wilson if you need anything," Mom said. She brushed Callie's wild hair out of her face.

"I won't need him," Callie whispered to Miss Kitty. "I don't need anybody. I'm almost nine."

Callie sat on the window seat in her room with Miss Kitty. She was writing to her best friend, Meghan Johnson, and Mr. Kitty. Mr. Kitty was Meghan's cat and came from the same litter as Miss Kitty. The two cats looked exactly alike.

Callie looked up from her letter and out the window. She saw the boy from church standing in *her* yard.

"Oh no, Miss Kitty. There he is!" Callie exclaimed. "I hope he doesn't think I want to play with him. 'Cause I don't." Callie and Miss Kitty hid behind the curtains and peeked out.

A minute later, David knocked on Callie's door and came in. "Cal," David called, "you in here? There's someone downstairs to see you."

"Tell him I can't come out," Callie yelled from behind the curtains. "Tell him anything! Just make him go away. He's a *boy*!"

"Callie, come on." David tried to pull Callie from her room and down the stairs. "You can't stay in your room forever."

"David Paul Davies," Callie warned, "you better let me go right now, or I'll tell Mom as soon as she gets back. You'll be in big trouble."

"Fine. Stay in your room with that cat. See if I care." David let go of Callie's arm and went back downstairs.

"Fine then, I will," Callie called after him. "Go back out with Jenni Wilson. I hope you marry her! I don't care."

With that, she slammed her bedroom door.

⚜⚜⚜

Later that afternoon, Callie and Miss Kitty came downstairs for dinner. She heard Mom and Daddy talking in low voices. Last time that happened, they had to move here. Now what?

When Daddy saw Callie, he and Mom stopped talking.

"Callie," Mrs. Davies said, "David told us the little boy from next door came over this afternoon. He said you wouldn't even go out to say hello."

"Mom," Callie whined, "he's a *boy*, and boys are so weird."

"Callie Ann." Daddy looked over the top of his glasses at Callie. "David is also a boy, you know."

"Yes, Daddy." Callie smiled. "And I rest my case! Boys are weird."

"Someday, Miss Callie, you won't think boys are weird." Mom gave Callie a hug.

"Someday, I guess." Callie leaned her face against her Mom's neck. "Someday."

❦❦❦

"His name is Jason Alexander, Cal," David said. He and Callie were sitting on the screened porch, looking out over the backyard. "He seems real nice. I think you'd like him. He even has a cat. You know, Cal, it upsets Mom when you won't even try to make friends."

"David," Callie began in a serious voice. She turned to look at her brother. "Why did we have to leave Greenville? I mean, I prayed real hard and asked God to please let us stay. I miss all the people we grew up with—Grandmama and Papa and Meghan and Mr. Kitty. I guess God didn't hear me. I guess He was busy." Callie looked away so David couldn't see her tears.

"Callie, you're silly!" David pulled his little sister closer to him. "God hears us no matter where we are. He had plans for us here. That's all, Callie. He didn't move us to make you unhappy. He just needed all of us here. You'll get used to Cornelius."

David got up out of the swing they had been sitting in. "Good night, Callie."

Callie gave David a big hug and said goodnight.

"Come on, Miss Kitty. I guess you and I need to go in, too," she said as she picked up the snoozing cat.

❧❧❧

Brushing her hair before going to bed, Callie talked to Miss Kitty. The cat was lying on her bed. "I still don't understand why God needed us here. David says it will be OK. But I just don't know." Callie turned off the lights and got into bed. Miss Kitty climbed in beside her. "I just don't know."

Chapter Two

THE NEXT MORNING, CALLIE'S DADDY was in his study when Callie and Miss Kitty came down for breakfast. "Well, good morning, sleepyheads." He gave Callie a kiss on the forehead and Miss Kitty a rub on the head. "Your mom had to go to the store this morning, and David's already gone. So it's just us for breakfast," he said as they walked into the kitchen. "What do you think you'd like?"

"Could I please have peanut butter toast?" Callie put Miss Kitty in the chair by the kitchen window. "Daddy, I don't think Miss Kitty feels good today. Could we just stay up in our room?"

"Well, Callie," Daddy said as he fixed Callie her toast, "I was thinking that you haven't had your bike out yet. Why don't you and I take Miss Kitty over to the church so she can look around? I have some work I could do while we're over there. And you could use the fresh air."

Callie really didn't want to go, but she couldn't think of a reason not to. "Sure, Daddy, that would be fine."

After breakfast, Callie and Miss Kitty went back upstairs so Callie could get dressed. Daddy would get the bikes out of the barn in the backyard.

Just as they were getting ready to go, the boy from next door came running across the backyard.

"Hi, Reverend Davies. Remember me?" He yelled at the top of his voice. "I'm Jason Alexander. I live next door."

"Yes, Jason, I do remember you." Callie's father smiled. "This is Callie, our daughter, and her cat, Miss Kitty. We are going to ride our bikes over to the church," he said as he put on his bike helmet. "Would you like to come with us?"

"Great! Let me ask Mom." Jason raced across the yard to his house.

"DADDY," Callie said in a loud voice. "He

can't come with us. He's a boy! And Miss Kitty don't like boys." Callie was trying to think of anything to keep Jason from coming with them.

"*Doesn't*, Callie. *Doesn't* like boys. And yes, Miss Kitty does. I'm a boy, and she likes me," Daddy said.

"Don't be silly." Callie put Miss Kitty in the basket on her bike. "Daddies are not real boys. Besides, I don't want to have to play with him."

Jason came around the house with his bike. "Mom said I could go if it's OK with you, Reverend Davies!" He almost ran into the clothesline.

"Fine with me, Jason." Callie's daddy smiled.

Funny, Callie thought as she looked at her daddy. *He's smiling just like David does when he's up to something*. Maybe Daddy was a real boy after all.

As the three of them started to pedal down the driveway, Mom returned from the store. "Hi," she said as they passed. "Where are y'all going?"

"Just over to the church," Callie's father answered as they went on. "We'll be back by lunch."

"Why are we taking that cat to see the church?" Jason asked Callie as they turned down Smith street. "I mean, cats don't go to church or anything."

"For your information—"

"Callie," her daddy said in a tone of voice that meant *be nice*!

"Well," Callie started again. "Miss Kitty was born in our church at home. She liked to play there while Daddy did his paper work." She pedaled her bike faster, trying to outride Jason.

"At home?" Jason asked as he pedaled faster, too. "You mean y'all are not staying?"

"We're staying," Callie's daddy said, huffing and puffing. "Callie's just a little homesick. She hasn't met very many people here yet."

"Oh," Jason said.

Callie could tell Jason was having a hard time keeping up with her. *Good*, she thought. *Maybe he'll go home.*

As Callie turned onto Riverbend Road, she could see the church. She didn't remember all the really pretty flowers in the yard or that it was this big. She still didn't like it, though.

"Daddy," Callie said as she slowed down

enough for him to catch her. "David said God hears us no matter where we are. Is he right?"

"He's right, Callie—no matter where you are or who you are." They reached the parking lot and stopped.

Once they got inside the church, Reverend Snow came up. "Well, hello!" he said in a loud voice. "Miss Callie, I'm glad you're here. I wanted to tell you how sorry I am for not saying your name right yesterday. I'm old, and unless I write names down, I forget." He gave Callie a pat on the back and turned to her daddy. As the two men began to talk, Jason pulled Callie away.

"You'll really like it here," Jason said as he gave Callie a tour of all the best hiding places in the church. "We have lots of things to do. You can go swimming or hiking or just about anything else."

"Do you have a mall?" Callie asked. "I haven't seen one yet. Back home, we have three malls and a water park."

"Well—we have a few shops downtown, and you can go to Statesville to the mall," Jason said as he showed Callie the hiding place under the basement steps. "I don't know what a water park is, but we have a creek out back of the church."

Callie stared at him in surprise. *How can he not know what a water park is? Boys sure aren't too smart!*

"Come on, Callie. I want to show you the bell tower." Jason ran ahead of Callie and her cat. "You want me to hold your cat for a while? She looks awfully heavy! I have a cat. His name is Jack, and he's all white."

"No thank you. Miss Kitty don't—*doesn't* like boys." Callie shifted her twenty-pound cat from one side to the other. "Are we supposed to be going up here?"

"Sure. Reverend Snow don't mind as long as we're careful." Jason turned to look back down the steps at Callie. "Hurry up! You can see the whole town. Hey, I can see your house—mine, too."

"Oh my! You really can see the whole town from here!" Callie exclaimed when she caught up with Jason.

"Yep," said Jason proudly. "The whole town."

Chapter Three

"CALLIE! JASON!" CALLIE'S FATHER called. "You two need to come down now. Time to start home."

Callie took one long last look around at the small town. Cornelius was really a very pretty town. But it still wasn't home.

"Here, you carry Miss Kitty back down. She's getting heavy." Callie handed the big black cat to Jason.

"Fine by me. But I thought you said she didn't like boys." He took the cat from Callie and went to the door.

"Well . . . maybe she'll like you—if you hold her right." Callie double-checked to make sure he was.

They shut the door to the bell tower and went down the steps.

"You two sure are slow," Callie's father said as Callie and Jason came toward him. "My goodness, Jason, you look out of breath. Are you all right?"

"Yeah, I'm fine. This cat must weigh a ton." Jason put Miss Kitty over his shoulder.

"She does not weigh a ton!" Callie argued as they went out the back door of the church. "Give her to me."

With that, Callie put the cat in the basket on her bike.

On the ride back home, Jason talked nonstop. Callie couldn't even tell her daddy about how pretty Cornelius was from the bell tower.

"I have a cat, too, Reverend Davies. His name is Jack. We named him for the man who gave him to me for my birthday," Jason said without taking a breath.

"That's real nice, Jason." Callie's father turned to look at her. "Did you have a good time, Callie?"

"I guess so. Miss Kitty sure liked the church," Callie said as she rode close to her daddy. "I think she liked the bell tower best."

"How do you know that?" Jason gave her one of those weird boy looks. "Did she tell you?"

Callie pedaled faster then. She wanted to get in front of Jason and her daddy. She didn't want to talk to Jason any more today. As she rode, Callie thought, *What kind of name is Jack for a cat?* Oh, well. It was a *boy* cat. And it did belong to Jason.

"Callie, wait up. I want to show you the park!" Jason called from behind her.

"You go ahead, Jason. Miss Kitty and I are going home." Callie turned up the street to her house.

As Callie came in the back door of the old farmhouse, Mrs. Davies was hanging up the phone. "Hi there, sweetie. How was your ride?"

"It was fine, I guess. We had to take Jason Alexander with us, and all he did was talk. He has a cat, too. Guess what he named him, Mom? Jack, of all things! Who would name a cat Jack?" Callie opened the refrigerator, looking for something to drink.

"Hi, honey," Daddy said as he came in the back door. "Is lunch ready?"

"It sure is. We're having Callie's favorite, pizza." Mrs. Davies pulled the hot pizza out of the oven. "You two need to wash up before we eat. Callie, will you call David as you go up?"

"Sure, Mom." Callie ran up the steps.

"Slow down, young lady, before you break your neck," her daddy called after her.

"David, Mom said to call you for lunch." Callie stuck her head in her brother's room. "We're having pizza, so you'd better get there before I do."

"Sure, Cal. I'll have it half gone before you even get down the steps," David said as he passed her in the doorway. "Girls are so slow."

"I'll show you," Callie said, squeezing by David on the stairs. She forgot to wash her hands.

Callie got to the table just as her mom was putting the pizza in the center.

"Callie, will you say the blessing?" Daddy asked.

"Yes, sir," Callie said. "Dear God, thank you for the food we are about to eat. And thank you for this wonderful day. I even thank you for David, even if he is a boy. Amen."

"Well, Callie, that was nice of you." David laughed. "And I thank God for you, too! I'm *really* thankful you weren't twins."

Callie pretended she hadn't heard him. "Mom, when I came in, you were on the phone. You said you'd see somebody on Saturday. Are you going somewhere?" Her mom had to know Saturday was Callie's birthday. Callie hoped Mom didn't have to go somewhere on that day.

"It's not nice to listen to other people's phone calls, Miss Callie Ann. But no, I'm not going anywhere Saturday." Mrs. Davies gave Callie a stern look. "I have some errands to do downtown Wednesday, though."

Mom's answer did not tell Callie anything about what Mom was planning for her birthday. But she dropped it for now. Mom was up to something. But what? Maybe David knew. She'd ask him later.

"Callie and Jason took Miss Kitty up to the bell tower this morning," Daddy said.

"Oh, really? Was it pretty up there, Callie?" Mom asked.

"Yeah, Mom, it was so neat. You can see the whole town. And you can see our house and

Jason's from there. Oh, and did you know that there is a creek right behind the church?" Callie wanted to tell her mom everything all at once. "And flowers, Mom—lots and lots of flowers."

"Slow down, Cal," David said. "How did you get into the bell tower?"

"Jason Alexander showed me where the steps are. Want me to show you tomorrow?" Callie was so excited, she almost spilled her milk.

"I don't know. Jenni Wilson and I planned to walk to the high school tomorrow." David got up and put his plate in the sink.

"But, David," Callie whined. "I want you to go riding with me."

"I'm sure Jason would love to ride with you, Callie. He seems like a nice boy," Daddy said.

"But, Daddy, he's a *boy*!" Callie sighed. Didn't her daddy know she couldn't be friends with a boy?

Chapter Four

THE NEXT DAY WAS TUESDAY. After lunch, Callie watched as her father met Jason under an old tree in his yard.

"Sure, Reverend Davies, I'd love to go for a ride. As long as Callie don't mind."

This is awful, Callie thought. Her daddy was asking Jason Alexander to ride bikes with her! Back home, she wouldn't have had to ask a boy to ride with her. She would have had Meghan and Mr. Kitty. But here in Cornelius, all she had was a boy.

"I guess it could be worse," she told herself. "But I don't know how."

Jason and Callie climbed on their bikes and

rode down their street. They passed David and Jenni Wilson.

"Y'all watch for cars!" David called after the two of them. "Do you hear me, Cal?"

"I will, David," Callie called back as she and Jason went up the hill to the school.

"This is our school, Callie. This is were you'll be going in September." Jason got off his bike. They could almost see Callie's house from the school.

"It's so big. How many grades are here?" Callie got off her bike, too, and took off her helmet.

"Oh, we go first through eighth at this school. Then high school," Jason explained as he bent down to tie his shoe.

"Eight grades in one school?!" Callie almost yelled it. "Back home, we have only three!"

"I wish you'd stop saying that." Jason hopped up the steps to the school.

"Saying what?" Callie put her hands on her hips and gave Jason her meanest look.

"Back home. I mean, you are home. Your mom and daddy are here, and so is your brother.

So you are home." Jason gave her a mean look right back.

"Well, it doesn't feel like home," Callie said. "I'm having a birthday at the end of the week, and nobody here knows it. Everybody at home always did. And they all cared."

"Give us time, Callie. You haven't even been here a week," Jason said back. "We're not that bad, if you'll just give us a chance. I think you're spoiled!" He was shouting now.

With that, Callie hopped on her bike and raced back down the street.

"Who does Jason think he is?" Callie said to herself as she came up behind David and Jenni. "I don't need him. I don't need anybody."

"Hey, Cal! What's wrong?" David called as Callie sped past them. "Hey, wait up!"

When David caught up to Callie, she was sitting under the shade tree at the end of their street, crying. He sat down beside her.

"Oh, come on, Cal. What's wrong? Are you hurt?" he asked.

Callie didn't answer. She couldn't stop crying.

"Come on now, don't cry." He put his arm around her.

Callie and David had always been close. She knew he loved her even if sometimes he didn't act like it. But he couldn't help her now.

"Tell me what's wrong. I'll listen, Cal. I always have." He pulled his arm back and looked into her face.

"I don't like it here. I want to go back to Greenville. Back to where I know people. Please, David, please talk to Mom and Daddy. Make 'em see we need to go back." All her words fell out at once.

"Cal, calm down. You know we can't do that," David said. "Now, what's really going on? Come on, tell me."

"My birthday is this week, David. I heard Mom on the phone this morning telling somebody that she'd see them Saturday. That means she forgot my birthday. And just as bad, my school here will have eight grades in it. My school back home had only three. And I knew most of the people there." Callie sniffed, trying not to cry.

David put his arm back around Callie.

"Things change, Callie. We have to be here, so we need to make the best of it. And there's no way Mom forgot your birthday. Mom never forgets. She may be up to something, but no way did she forget." He smiled at Callie and wiped a tear off her face.

"You don't know what's she's up to?" Callie was much calmer now.

"Sorry, Callie. I can't help you with that one. But I can tell you that Mom never forgets. Come on, I'll walk you home." David held out a hand to his sister.

"No thank you, David. I'll go by myself. I'll be fine, really." Callie stayed under the shade tree.

"You're sure? You know I'll be happy to go with you. Jenni and I can go see the school anytime."

"You go ahead and catch Jenni. I'll be fine. Anyway, here comes Jason. I think I have to say I'm sorry for running off." Callie gave David a weak smile.

Jason really was a nice person, even if he was a boy. And Callie didn't have anyone else to talk to. Jason was looking more like a friend than just another boy.

"Callie!" Jason was out of breath from trying to catch up with her. "I'm sorry. I really am. It's just that I'm trying really hard to be your friend, and you won't let me. Don't you want to make new friends?" Jason sat down under the tree beside Callie and gave her a sad puppy dog look.

"I'm sorry, too, Jason. It's just that I've never lived anywhere except Greenville. I miss all the people and our old house. I really miss home." Callie looked down at her shoes.

"But, Callie, you *are* at home," Jason said, smiling.

"Have you ever lived anywhere else?" Callie asked.

"Sure. My dad was in the army, so we've lived lots of other places. I was born in England." He pulled a blade of grass.

"England? The England in Europe?" Callie opened her eyes wide.

"Well, as far as I know, that's the only England. So yeah. Dad is an army recruiter now, so I guess we'll be here for a while," Jason said, playing with the grass he had pulled.

Callie liked the way Jason smiled when he talked. But he was still a boy!

"Callie, as long as you have your parents and David, you'll be OK here." Jason squinted his blue eyes up at the sun.

"You're right, Jason. Cornelius is really not that bad. It's even kinda pretty. And I do have Mom and Daddy with me. Maybe I'll be fine here." Callie got up to get her bike. "Could you show me the school again?"

"Sure." Jason hopped up and was on his bike before Callie could get to hers.

Chapter Five

CALLIE AND JASON COASTED INTO the school lot and parked their bikes in front of the school building. They raced up the steps.

"Wow, this place is bigger than I thought! Are we supposed to be in here?" Callie asked as they went in the school's huge front doors.

"It's all right. My mom is here working. She's a teacher. She said I could bring you over if you wanted to see the place." Jason pulled Callie down the hall.

As Callie and Jason passed the office, a very tall man came out.

"Hi there, Jason," he said. "Who do you have with you?"

Jason stopped. "Hello, Mr. Tucker. This is

Callie Davies, the new preacher's daughter. And, Callie, this is the best principal in the whole world, Mr. Tucker."

"Well, hello, Callie. It's nice to meet you. My family didn't get to meet you at church on Sunday. We were in Greenville." Mr. Tucker shook Callie's hand.

"Greenville! We moved here from Greenville," Callie said. "My best friend in the whole world lives there. Her name is Meghan Johnson."

He grinned. "Yes, I know. Meg told me all about you while I was there. She's my niece." A telephone rang in the office. "I'd better get that. Jason, your mom is in her new room—next to Mrs. Smith's." Mr. Tucker hurried back into the office to get the phone.

As Callie and Jason went down the hall, they passed a huge library. Callie loved to read. It didn't matter what book it was. She and Meghan used to have reading contests back home to see who could read the most books. Meghan always seemed to win, but only by a little.

"Hi, honey," Mrs. Alexander said as Callie and Jason walked into her classroom. "And this must be Callie. How are you?"

"I'm just fine, Mrs. Alexander. How are you?" Callie looked around the room. *Mrs. Alexander must teach math*, she thought.

"I'm fine, Callie. Thank you for asking. Have you two had lunch yet?" Jason's mom sat on the desk beside Jason.

"Yes, ma'am," Jason answered. "I've been showing Callie around the school."

"Boy, is it ever big!" Callie said. "Back home—I mean, my old school wasn't near this big. I hope I don't get lost." Callie looked up at Mrs. Alexander.

"You won't, Callie. I'm here to help you." Jason grinned.

"Well, I need a break. So if y'all would like to go with me to have my lunch, I'll treat you to an ice cream." Mrs. Alexander gathered her papers and put them in a bag.

"I'd love to go, Mrs. Alexander. I need to call my mom first to see if it's all right," Callie said.

"Here, Callie. You can use Mom's phone." Jason reached into his mom's work bag and pulled out a small phone. "Neat, huh?"

"Wow, this is neat." Callie looked at the

phone in Jason's hand. "Can you use it any-where?"

"Sure can. Mom called me from the store last night to see if I wanted pizza." Jason handed the phone to Callie.

Callie dialed her number. Funny, she already was having a hard time remembering the number she had in Greenville.

When her mom answered, Callie said, "Mom, this is Callie. Jason and I stopped by the school to see his mom. She wants to know if I can go for ice cream with her and Jason."

"I think that would be real nice of Mrs. Al-exander," Mom said. "Could I please speak to her first?"

Callie handed the phone to Mrs. Alexander. "She wants to talk to you."

"Hello, Mrs. Davies," Jason's mom said. "This is Carol Alexander. How are you?"

Mrs. Alexander was quiet while she listened to Callie's mom.

"It's nice talking with you, too. I'll tell Callie to check in with you after we get back." Mrs. Alexander gave Jason and Callie the thumbs-up sign.

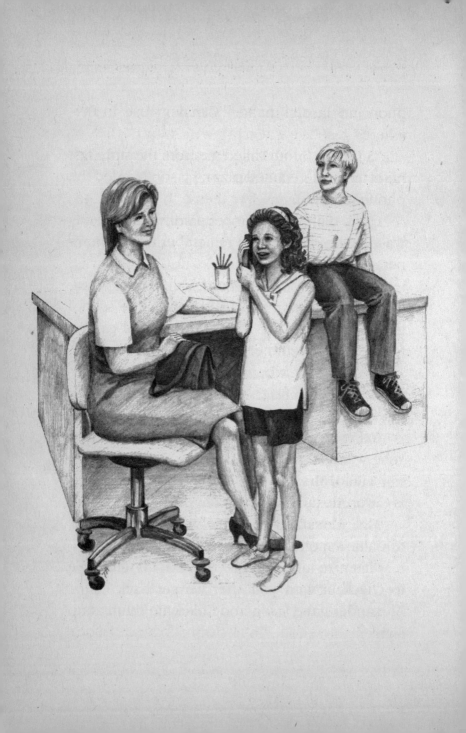

"Come on, Callie. We'll put our bikes in the bike rack so we can ride with Mom." Jason pulled Callie out of Mrs. Alexander's room and down the hall to the front door.

A voice boomed after them. "It was nice to meet you, Callie. We look forward to having you at our school next year."

Callie smiled back at Mr. Tucker, who was standing in the door of the office. "Thank you, sir. I look forward to being here." *I think.*

❧❧❧

After they had their ice cream, Mrs. Alexander drove Callie and Jason back to school to pick up their bikes.

"You two be careful," Mrs. Alexander said as she got out of the car. "Callie, remember to check in with your mom. Jason, I'll be home around three, and so will your dad. OK?"

"OK, Mom. See ya then," Jason said as they climbed on their bikes.

"Thank you for the ice cream, Mrs. Alexander," Callie called back over her shoulder.

As Callie and Jason rode back down the big hill from the school, Callie turned to him. "Jason, we're friends now, right?" she asked in her most serious voice.

"I guess so." Jason gave Callie an unsure look. "Why do you ask?"

"Well, friends help each other. And I need some help. You see," Callie explained, "my birthday is Saturday. I think Mom is up to something. I don't know what. David doesn't even know."

They stopped at the shade tree where they had been earlier.

"And?" Jason got off his bike and sat against the tree trunk.

"And I need your help to find out what she's up to." Callie sat down beside Jason.

"What ya want me to do, spy on her?" Jason said in a loud voice.

"Well—yes, I guess so. It wouldn't take you long. She said she has things to do in the morning in town. You could just see where she goes." Callie had it all planned out.

"Callie Davies, you really want me to spy on your mom?" Jason was almost yelling.

"Hush!" Callie looked around to see if anybody could hear them. "It really wouldn't be spying. You'd just be looking out for her. I just want to know if she's forgotten my birthday. That's all." She gave Jason her best lost puppy look.

"Don't look at me with sad eyes, Callie Ann. Oh, all right. I'll do it. I won't like it, but I'll help you."

"Thanks, Jason." Callie climbed on her bike. "I'll see you tomorrow morning, then."

❧❧❧

At dinner that evening, Callie's mom talked about her plans for the next morning. "I think I'll walk to town. The weatherman said it's going to rain, but not till tomorrow evening."

"What time are you leaving, Mom?" Callie asked.

"Oh, about nine, I guess," Mom answered.

After helping with the dishes, Callie went up to her room to write Meghan. But then she saw her cat. "Oh, Miss Kitty, I'm sorry I was gone all day. But I have a lot to tell you."

Callie told Miss Kitty all her and Jason's plans. She said her prayers when she was ready for bed. "Dear God, thank you for sending me

Jason, even if he is a boy. He's nice. Bless everyone I know and even people I don't know. And
please don't be mad at me for spying on Mom. I
just have to know what's going on. Good night,
God. Amen."

Callie turned off the lights, pulled Miss Kitty
up to the pillow, and fell sound asleep.

Chapter Six

EARLY WEDNESDAY MORNING, Callie heard something outside the window. "What in the world could that be this early?" Callie said to Miss Kitty, who was looking at her with wide eyes. Then Callie heard someone call her name from outside. It sounded like it came from the pecan tree.

"Callie, you up?" Jason called. "Come to the window."

"Jason?" Callie opened the window. "What are you doing in the tree?"

"Well, I guess I could have walked in your house to wake you. But I don't think your mom and dad would have liked that. Anyway, what time is your mom leaving?" Jason asked, hanging on to a tree limb.

"About nine or so. Why?" Callie sat on the window seat and put Miss Kitty in her lap.

"Just get dressed and come down. I've got something to show you." Jason climbed down from the tree.

Callie got dressed in such a hurry she forgot to brush her hair. She picked up Miss Kitty and ran down the stairs.

Daddy was sitting at the kitchen table reading the morning paper. "You two sure are up early. Going out to play with Jason?"

"No, sir. He just wants to show me something," Callie said. "Is it OK if I go out for a minute?"

"Sure. I'll start breakfast while you see what he wants," he said.

"Jason, where are you?" Callie called as she and Miss Kitty came out the back door.

"Here I am, Callie, over by the tree." Jason waved.

"What did you want to show me?" Callie looked around. Could her daddy see them from the back door?

"Look—walkie talkies. This way when I'm following your mom, you'll know where we are!" Jason had a big grin on his face.

"ALL RIGHT! Jason, you're wonderful."

Jason blushed bright red. "Anyway," he went on, "this way you can hear what she's up to."

"You're so smart." Callie gave Jason a quick hug. Miss Kitty gave her a look of surprise.

"Let's try 'em before she leaves. You go back to your room, and I'll call you." Jason walked toward his yard.

"OK," Callie picked up Miss Kitty and ran back into the house.

"I'll be right back down," she said to her daddy as she passed through the kitchen.

As soon as Callie was in her room and had the door shut, she went to her window. Jason was in the backyard.

"Jason to base, come in base," his voice crackled over the walkie talkie.

"I'm here, Jason. This is great." Then she said in a low voice, "My mom should be leaving in a few minutes. Talk to you later."

Callie's daddy called her down to eat. "Be down in a minute," she called back.

Callie's mom was going into the kitchen as Callie came down the steps for breakfast.

"Good morning, Callie," her mom said as Callie sat down. "What are you up to today?"

Callie looked at her mom, trying not to look guilty of anything. "Why do you ask?"

"Well, you're up very early. And you've already been out to talk to Jason. I thought you two might be going to ride bikes," Mom said.

"Oh no. Jason has to go somewhere this morning," Callie said. "I'll just clean my room or something until he gets back."

"Clean your room!" Daddy exclaimed. "Oh my, honey. We might want to call the doctor to see if Callie's sick!"

"Oh, Daddy, you're silly," Callie giggled.

Callie was quiet while she ate her breakfast. She hoped her parents didn't suspect anything.

When she was done, she got up from the table to go upstairs. "I'm going up now. Have a good time in town, Mom."

Callie ran back up to her room and closed the door. "Base to Jason, come in Jason," Callie said into the walkie talkie. "Mom's leaving now. Can you see her?"

"Got her, base. Catch you later. Over and out." Jason waved to her from behind the old pecan tree.

Callie knew it would be a while before he called her back. She started cleaning her room. As she was making her bed, Miss Kitty jumped onto the pillow. Callie picked up the cat. "Miss Kitty, I wonder if Mom has forgotten my birthday."

"Jason to base." Jason's voice came over the walkie talkie. "Where are ya, Callie?"

"I'm here, Jason! Where are you?" Callie kept her voice low.

"At the old soda shop on Main Street. Your mom's at the beauty shop next door," Jason said.

"What's she doing there?" Callie asked. She looked at Miss Kitty, who was sniffing the walkie talkie in Callie's hand.

"Well, if I had to guess, I'd say getting her hair done. Whatcha think she's doing?"

"Funny, Jason, real funny," Callie said. "Mom just had her hair done the other day. Keep watching her. What's she doing now?"

"She's using the phone."

Just then, Callie heard her own phone ring.

"Hang on a minute, Jason," she said. "Our phone just rang." Callie poked her head out her bedroom door and heard her dad answer the phone.

"Oh, hi, honey," he said. "How are the plans coming?"

Callie almost screamed into the walkie talkie, "She's talking to my daddy! Get closer. Can you hear what she's saying?" Callie picked up Miss Kitty and paced her room.

"I don't think I'll be able to," Jason answered in a loud whisper. "It's hard to see your mom without her seeing me. Hold on. The door's open. I'll try to crawl around the side here and listen."

"Be careful," Callie said into the radio. "All we need is for Mom to see you with the walkie talkie."

Waiting to hear from Jason again, Callie sat on her bed, biting her nails. Several minutes passed. She got up and paced some more. She wished she were there with Jason. She wanted to know what on earth was going on.

"Jason, what's happening? I can't stand not knowing another minute," Callie almost yelled

into the walkie talkie after fifteen minutes had passed.

"You can relax, Callie. Your mom went into the back of the shop a while ago," Jason said. "I think she's getting something done to her hair."

"But I told you she had her hair done the other day. She can't be having it done again." Callie was tired of explaining that to Jason.

"Don't tell me. *I'm* the one sitting under the window waiting for her. And I tell you, she's in the back of the shop with Mrs. Stevens." Jason sounded as if he was a little tired of waiting.

A long time went by. Jason must have left his walkie talkie on, because Callie heard noises from the street. Then Callie heard a familiar voice.

"Hello, Jason." It was Callie's mom! "What are you doing here?"

Chapter Seven

CALLIE HEARD NOTHING FOR A MOMENT. She hoped Jason didn't give away their plan!

Then she heard him say, "I . . . well . . . I'm just going home. Yeah, that's it. I'm going home."

"Great, Miss Kitty," Callie moaned. "Mom will find out for sure now that I had Jason follow her."

"Well, Jason," Callie heard her mom say. "I'm going home, too. Let's walk together."

"Oh no!" Callie picked up her cat. "We're doomed now! Really doomed."

Then Callie heard her mom ask Jason about the radio in his pocket.

"Well, you see, Mrs. Davies, it's not really a

radio. I mean, it is, but not for music." Jason was falling all over his words.

"Now we're really in for it!" Callie said out loud to herself. She grabbed Miss Kitty and headed out of her room. She almost knocked David off his feet as she ran past.

"Hey, hey! Where are you two going in such a hurry?" David exclaimed.

"Out!" Callie called back. She and Miss Kitty raced down the steps and out the back door.

"Hi, Mom, Jason! Where have you two been?" Callie ran to meet her mom and Jason at the end of the driveway. She gave Jason a sharp look.

"Well, let me see . . . I went to pay a few bills, then I stopped in at Mason's Dress Shop. Oh! And the beauty shop." Mrs. Davies smiled at Callie. "Why do you ask?"

"Oh, no reason. No reason at all. Would it be OK if Jason and I went bike riding?" Callie asked, staring at her mom's hair. It looked the same to her. What had Mom been up to at the beauty shop?

"Fine with me, Callie. I'll take Miss Kitty back into the house with me," Mrs. Davies said. "You two have fun. Come on, Kitty, let's go inside."

Callie and Jason walked next door to get Jason's bike and to drop off his walkie talkie. "I can't believe you left the walkie talkie on and Mom didn't catch us," Callie said.

"Did her hair look like that this morning?" Jason got his bike from the back porch.

"I guess. I don't know. Mom's hair always looks the same to me." Callie put on her bike helmet. "Besides, you were the one following her. Did it look any different to you?"

"Not really. But she sure was in there a long time. Maybe she had to get a perm or something." Jason shrugged as they pedaled up the hill.

"Jason, she has curly hair. Why would she want a perm?" Callie stared at him as if he were from outer space. "Besides, Mom never has anything done to her hair except haircuts."

"Well, I don't know, Callie. She was in there for a while." Jason slowed down and asked, "Where is the other walkie talkie?"

"Oh no! It's in my room. Come on. I'll go in the side door and get it." Callie turned her bike around and started back home. They parked their bikes in the front yard and walked around to the side of the house. "I'll be right back, Jason. Watch for Mom or Daddy!" Callie warned as she went in the side door.

She went quickly up the steps and into her room. Coming back down, she could see Mom on the phone. Callie stopped to listen. Who was she talking to? Callie heard Mr. Tucker's name. Why was Mr. Tucker calling her house?

Callie went back out the side door. She ran around the house to where Jason was waiting. "Jason, Mom's on the phone with Mr. Tucker!" She was out of breath. "What in the world could Mr. Tucker be calling *my* house for? School hasn't started yet. And I didn't do anything."

"I don't know, Callie. Maybe he's calling about next school year." Jason picked up his bike. "Did you hear anything else she said?"

"No, I just got out of there fast. I didn't want her to see me with your walkie talkie." Callie followed Jason through the yard to his house.

"Well, don't worry about it then. I'm sure if it's about you, she'll tell you." Jason put the walkie talkie with the other one.

Don't worry about it? Boys were all the same.

Mom had to be up to something. Callie just had to find out what it was! They started back up the hill.

"Jason, you're sure Mom stayed in the beauty shop the whole time?" Callie gave Jason a hard look. "Her hair didn't look any different to me."

"Callie, I'm telling you for the millionth time." Jason sounded upset. "She went in. She stayed for a while. She came out and saw me. Then she asked what I was doing downtown."

"But you didn't tell her, did you?" Callie asked.

"Sure, Callie. What, you think I'm dumb or something? Besides, the walkie talkie was on, and you heard everything. I couldn't tell on you without telling on myself. And this wasn't even my idea." Jason threw up his hands so hard he almost fell off his bike.

"Well . . ." Callie pulled on a red curl. "I really don't think you're dumb. It's just that Mom already had her hair done this week. I don't know why she'd go back in." She gave Jason an "I'm sorry" look.

"Maybe—just *maybe*—she had it done again. You know, for something special!" Jason said as they stopped under the shade tree at the end of the street.

"Maybe. But why did Mr. Tucker call my house? I didn't think he and my mom even knew each other." Callie was worried.

"Here we go again. You could worry the fuzz off of a caterpillar, Callie." Jason sat up. "Just wait and see if she says anything."

"OK, OK." Callie looked up at the dark clouds in the sky. "Looks like it might rain. I guess we'd better go back home."

"Sure. Wanna race?" Jason hopped on his bike.

"See you at home!" Callie called as she passed Jason.

Callie just made it home before the rain started. "See you later, Jason," she called from her back porch. She heard voices in the kitchen. But as she went in the screen door, it got real quiet. Callie could tell Mom and Daddy had been talking about something they didn't want her to hear. And David looked like he had just had a good laugh. Maybe all of them were up to something.

"Hi, sweetie." Daddy stood up from the table. "Looks like you made it in just in time."

"I did, Daddy. But I didn't have time to put my bike in the barn. So I just put it on the porch." Callie poured herself a glass of milk.

"That's all right, Callie. I'll put it up when I go out." David gave his sister a big grin. "I have to get something out of the barn anyway."

"Thanks, David. What do you need out there?" Callie asked.

"Oh, just something Mom wants. Nothing major." David put his lunch plate in the sink and went out the door.

That's it, Callie thought. They were *all* in on it. But what was it?!

Chapter Eight

TWO NIGHTS LATER, DAVID AND CALLIE sat on the back screen porch. "David," Callie said, "do you know what tomorrow is?"

"Sure, Cal. It's Saturday. I'm going over to the Wilsons' pool and then to a cookout with Jenni." David turned toward Callie. "Why? Do you have something planned?"

"I guess not," Callie said sadly.

"Well, I'm going to bed. Good night." David stood up to go in the house. "Hope the bed bugs don't carry you away while you're sleeping."

"Good night, David," Callie said softly.

Callie picked up her cat. "That does it, Miss Kitty. They don't have anything planned for my ninth birthday. June fourteenth will be just another day. David can't keep secrets. He would have told me by now." She held Miss Kitty in front of her. "Well, at least you love me, don't you, Miss Kitty?"

As Callie turned off the outside light, she could see Jason's light on in his room next door. *I wonder if he's telling me everything?*

Getting ready for bed, Callie could hear Mom and Daddy talking in low voices. It was just like the way they had talked back home, before they moved. *Please don't let it be another surprise like that one.* Leaving Greenville had been the worst thing Callie could remember happening in her life.

"Don't even think anything like that, Callie Ann," she said to herself. "Miss Kitty, come on. We need to say our prayers and go to bed. I have a feeling tomorrow is going to be a long day." Callie pulled the big cat on the bed and folded her hands to pray. "Dear God, I know this sounds selfish, but please don't let Mom and Daddy forget my birthday. And please bless everyone I know and even the ones I don't. Good night, God. Amen."

June fourteenth started as a very hot day and was getting hotter every minute. Callie had gotten up real early and sneaked downstairs to see if Mom and Daddy had left anything in the kitchen for her.

"Just as I thought, Miss Kitty," Callie said as she came back to her bedroom. "Nothing. Not one thing. No cards. Nothing. They did forget! Mom always left something when we were back home."

Miss Kitty cuddled closer to Callie.

"Callie, you up?" David knocked on Callie's bedroom door and peeked in. "Just wanted to say happy birthday before I headed off for the day. You been crying or what?"

"No . . . well, not really." Callie hid her eyes. "You have a good time. And thank you for the birthday wish."

"OK then. I'll see you later." David closed the door. Callie could hear him go down the back stairs and out the back door.

Callie and Miss Kitty moved over to the window seat. She could see David going down the street. "Fine then! Have a wonderful day. I'm sure I will, too," Callie said sadly as she waved back to her.

Mom and Daddy were finally up and having coffee when Callie went back down to the kitchen. Miss Kitty ran ahead of her.

"Good morning, Miss Kitty. And where is your owner this morning?" Daddy asked the cat. "There she is. Good morning, sweetie. What's with the sunglasses? Are you going out already?"

"Yes, sir. If it's all right with you and Mom." Callie kept her head low.

"Sure, honey. It's OK. You want to eat first?" Mrs. Davies asked.

"No, ma'am. I'd just like to go out for a while." Callie made her way to the back door. "Come on, Miss Kitty. You can go with me."

Callie could feel Mom watching her from the back door. Mom always watched Callie when she knew something was bothering her. Callie felt like running, but then Mom would know something was wrong. As Callie came around the house, she could see Jason headed for the pecan tree.

"Hi, Callie. What's with the sunglasses?"

"Nothing, just wanted to wear them," Callie snapped back.

"My, my. You're in a bad mood for a birthday girl!" Jason said as he sat on the ground.

"What birthday!? Nobody remembered but David. And he's gone to Jenni's for the day. Mom and Daddy just acted like nothing was going on." Callie sat down beside Jason and sniffed.

"Callie Davies, you've been crying." Jason looked at his friend.

"No . . . well, a little." Callie looked away so Jason couldn't see how red her eyes were.

"Callie, just wait and see what happens. Today isn't over yet. And there is still time for your mom to do almost anything." Jason gave Callie a pat on the arm. "You want to ride bikes later?"

"Yeah, I guess. I have to eat first and make up my bed." Callie pulled Miss Kitty to her.

"OK. Then I'll see you after you eat and all." Jason stood up. "Remember, Callie, today isn't over."

Callie got up and went to the back door to go inside. Mom and Daddy were talking in low voices again. Callie couldn't make out most of what they were saying—something about six o'clock.

As she went through the back door, Daddy asked Callie what she wanted to eat.

"I guess I'd like French toast, if that's not too much trouble?" Callie looked at both her parents. Why did they stop talking when she walked in a room?

"Nothing is too much trouble for my girl. Would you like milk with that?" Daddy had been the breakfast cook for as long as Callie could remember. Mom worked when they were back in Greenville. Daddy was the one who got her off to school and was there when she came home. Now, here in Cornelius, Mom and Daddy would both be home.

After they had breakfast, Callie took Miss Kitty upstairs for a nap. Miss Kitty loved to sleep in the bathtub after everyone had finished using it for the day.

"Here you go, Miss Kitty. You take your morning nap now. I'll be back this afternoon to take you outside. That way you can play with the pecans." Miss Kitty stretched out to sleep in the tub, and Callie went to her room.

"Callie, you in there?" Jason yelled in the window. "Are you ready to ride?"

Callie opened the window wider. "One of these days, Jason Alexander, you're going to break your neck climbing that old tree. I'm ready. Just let me pull my hair back." Callie closed the window and brushed her hair.

Back downstairs in the kitchen, Daddy was getting ready to go to the church for a while.

"Remember, honey, six o'clock," Callie's mom told Daddy.

"Are we having people over?" Callie asked from the kitchen doorway.

"Why do you ask?" Mrs. Davies turned around to see Callie.

Callie came all the way into the kitchen. "I just heard you tell Daddy to be home by six. I thought, maybe, that somebody was coming."

"Sorry, sweetie. I think it's just us. You and Jason be very careful while you're riding." Mrs. Davies gave Callie a hug.

But Callie couldn't stop wondering. She had heard six o'clock twice now. *What happens at six?*

Chapter Nine

CALLIE AND JASON RODE THEIR BIKES all around Cornelius. They stopped at the school to swing for a while.

"You know, Jason," Callie said. "I can't believe Mom, of all people, would forget my birthday." She tried to swing as high as she could.

"And I keep telling you the day isn't over yet. Just wait." Jason sounded as though he was tired of hearing about Callie's birthday.

Callie couldn't imagine Mom forgetting anything. She'd never forgotten the time Callie had thrown a baseball through the big window at Mrs. Cornwell's house. Or the time she hadn't done all her homework. Moms just never forgot. Never!

"It's almost lunchtime, Jason. You want to go to my house and have a picnic?" Callie asked.

"Sure. Will your mom care?" Jason slowed down to jump off the swing.

"No. She'll let us as long as we clean up our mess." Callie jumped off, too, and ran to her bike.

When Jason and Callie rode into the yard, they saw Callie's daddy pulling down the shades in the living room. What was he doing? Nobody ever went in there.

"Hi, Mom," Callie called as she and Jason walked in the back door. "Can Jason and I have a picnic under the old pecan tree?"

"Sure," Mom said. "What would you like to eat?" She looked around as if she was nervous.

"Peanut butter and jelly and Coke if we have any." Callie turned to see what her mom was looking at. She didn't see anything special.

"PBJs it is. Callie, you make those while I see if I can find some paper cups for you and Jason." Callie's mom went into the pantry, where she kept the cups and Coke.

That's funny, Callie thought. *Mom almost never lets me drink Coke in the middle of the day.*

"Can I help with anything?" Daddy said as he came into the kitchen. "Hi, Jason. What are y'all up to?"

"They're having a picnic. Doesn't that sound like fun?" Mom smiled nervously at Callie's daddy.

"PBJs all done," Callie said. "Daddy, I thought you were at the church!"

"Going right now. I just had to do something for your mom before she'd let me take off." He gave Callie a hug. "Y'all have a good lunch."

Callie watched her daddy back out of the drive. She and Jason would have to go over to the church after they ate lunch.

"Can you two make it OK? Or would you like my help?" Mom put the Cokes on the tray for Callie and Jason to carry outside.

"We've got it. Thanks, Mrs. Davies," Jason said. He went out the back door, Callie right behind him.

"They sure were acting strange," Callie said as they sat under the tree to eat. "Daddy acted like he was in a hurry to get back to church. After we eat, let's go see what he's up to."

"Sure, Callie. Anything you say." Jason rolled his eyes.

When they were done eating, Callie brought the tray and cups back into the kitchen. "Mom, Jason and I cleaned up our mess. Would it be all right if we rode over to the church to see Daddy?"

"I'm sure he'd love to have y'all come over," Callie's mom said. "Just make sure you're home before six o'clock."

There it was again. *What's so important about six o'clock?* Callie thought as they put on their bike helmets. She was sure going to find out, even if she had to wait till six o'clock.

As they biked up the hill, Jason asked Callie if she'd like an ice cream from the soda shop.

"That would be nice," Callie said. "But I don't have any money with me."

"Oh, it's OK," Jason said. "My mom pays them once a week for me to stop and get ice cream during the summer. They just take money for the ice cream from the account."

"That's great. I'll pay you back as soon as we get to the church," Callie said as they went into the store.

As soon as they had eaten their ice cream, Jason and Callie rode over to the church. Callie loved all the flowers out front.

"Hi, Daddy!" Callie said as she walked into the church study.

"Well, to what do I owe this honor?" Callie's daddy stood to give her a hug.

"Oh, we just wanted to look around like we did last time. Is that all right?" Callie looked around to see if anything was new in her daddy's study.

"Fine by me. Just be careful. I'll be in here if you need me." He sat back down in his big brown chair.

Jason showed Callie more hiding places. Then they went up to the bell tower and looked at the town. It didn't seem like they were there very long, but then Callie realized it was getting late.

"Jason, what time is it?" Callie jumped up. "Mom said six."

"It's ten till now," Jason said.

"Oh no!" Callie exclaimed. "If we don't hurry, we'll be late! We'd better get Daddy." She ran down the stairs.

Chapter Ten

CALLIE RAN INTO HER DADDY'S STUDY. "Daddy, we've got to go. Mom said we had to be home by six."

"Is it that time already? Y'all put your bikes in the car. You can ride with me." Her daddy stood up and turned off the study lights.

"OK, Daddy. We'll meet you at the car," Callie called as she went to get Jason.

As Jason and Callie waited at the car for her daddy, Callie thought, *Mom has never made us hurry home for dinner before. Daddy always works at the church as long as he needs to. So what's going on tonight?*

"You two ready? We wouldn't want to keep your mom waiting. Right, Callie?" Daddy got into the car and started toward home.

Everything looked the same when they pulled up. Nobody else's car was there. No flowers outside, no balloons. Just the same old house. *What's the hurry?* Callie wondered.

Inside, Mom was cooking dinner. David was still at Jenni's house. Even Miss Kitty was where Callie had left her, sleeping in the bathtub. Nothing was different. *There's nothing going on*, Callie thought. *Why did we have to be home by six o'clock?*

As Callie came down the steps, the front doorbell rang. "I'll get it, Mom," Callie called, going down the front hall to the door. Who could it be? Nobody ever came to the front door!

Opening the door, Callie saw Mr. Tucker. He was holding a cat that looked just like Miss Kitty. But Miss Kitty was upstairs in the tub asleep. "Hello, Mr. Tucker." Callie gave him a surprised look.

"Hello, Callie. Are your mom and daddy home?" Mr. Tucker smiled.

"Sure, come on in." Callie stood back from the door.

Just as Mr. Tucker moved, out from behind

him jumped Meghan! "Surprise, Callie! Happy Birthday!" Meghan grabbed Callie and gave her a big hug.

"MEGHAN, I can't believe it's you—really you!" Callie yelled at the top of her voice. She looked outside. Standing in her front yard was what looked like half the town.

"Oh, Mom! You didn't forget!" Callie ran to give her parents a big hug.

"Forget *your* birthday, Callie Ann? Never!" Daddy gave both Callie and Meghan a squeeze.

"I set it all up Wednesday morning," Mom said.

Callie was confused. "But I thought—"

"You thought I was in the beauty shop all that time, didn't you?" Mom smiled. "I knew you and Jason were up to something. So I slipped out the back door and went to the flower shop and bakery. I came back through the beauty shop. You and Jason never knew the difference."

"You really had us fooled," Callie said. "Thanks, Mom."

"Guess what, Callie?" Meghan was jumping up and down. "I can stay until Saturday!"

"Great, we'll have so much fun!" Callie spun

around and did a few ballet steps.

"Oh, Callie, you're such a dancer!" Meghan giggled, copying her friend. "Are you taking ballet here?" She stopped twirling and picked up Mr. Kitty. Callie should have known it was Mr. Kitty in Mr. Tucker's arms.

Callie had not even thought about dance class. "Oh, I'm sure Mom will find a class for me somewhere." She rolled her eyes.

Just then, David came in the door with Jenni. "Come outside, Callie. I have something you have to see." David pulled Callie out the front door. There, on the front porch, were nine pots of red tulips. Three flowers were in each pot. One pot for every year, just like when they were back in Greenville.

"I knew you were sad to leave your flowers in Greenville. So I thought you could just replace them here, in our new home." David gave Callie a big birthday hug.

"Callie Ann, come on in. Let's cut the cake," Daddy called from the living room.

"HAPPY BIRTHDAY, CALLIE!" everyone yelled as Callie blew out the nine candles on her cake.

Callie smiled. David was right—everything was going to be OK. *I guess now Cornelius really does feel like home, flowers and all!*

The End